THE MARSHAL OF ANGEL, TEXAS

A Western Adventure

Dylan Johnson

ISBN: 9781098752149

To:

Sarah-Lee, Marty, the Dodgers and Paw Paw – I love you all dearly.

About this novel

This new Western novel from Dylan Johnson will come as no surprise to the folks who have read his newspaper column. Yes, you may have read it too. Dylan Johnson is a pseudonym. Mister Johnson writes every single day—and this new book is the end result of a project he has had in mind for years. The Marshal of Angel, Texas was inspired by the great stories of J.C. Hulsey, who scored an immense hit with his first book "Angel Falls, Texas" a few years ago. He wishes to thank Mister Hulsey and hopes that you will enjoy this book—the first in a brand new series from a brand new Western writing talent.

Dedication

As a publishing company, we are always eager to find something new to offer our readers. We know that Western readers are some of the greatest in the world. The Western reader is one of the most loyal readers—a reader who will go through thick and thin to read their favorite authors. Take for example a gentleman I am very familiar with on our social media account. His passion for Westerns is unshakeable. His optimism is always welcome. He awaits not Kindle books—but paperbacks—paperback books! He's a Western fan. A hard-working, true, red-blooded gentleman of these United States. A man who isn't offended, isn't upset at the least little thing. He goes to work every single day selling his wares and comes home to read his Western novels. This book is dedicated to him. Thank you.

Foreword From Paul L. Thompson

The finest compliment another writer can pay an author is that he has come up with something new. Dylan Johnson has come up with something so new, so interesting, that I can't help but feel readers are going to enjoy it. This is the story of a small-town marshal who does something extraordinary. Well-written, entertainingly crafted. This is the first book in a series that readers are going to really find a lot they like about.

Paul L. Thompson – Bestselling author of the number one bestselling "U.S. Marshal: Shorty Thompson" series

Foreword From Robert Hanlon

Dylan Johnson is one of a new wave of authors—the kind of author readers will eagerly enjoy and await new releases from. He has the ability to truly understand what can be done differently, but reverently, with Westerns. Johnson, who comes from Texas, has already proven himself to me with this brand new adventure.

Robert Hanlon – Bestselling author of the number one bestselling "Timber: United States Marshal" series

CHAPTER ONE

"You have a good day now."

Kennedy looked back at the cook as he stuck the two extra biscuits in his pocket. "It's too nice outside not to have a good day. In fact, it looks like the makings of a great or perfect day, Charlie. But I thank you greatly and same to you."

The bell above the door clanged as Marshal John Kennedy stepped onto the boardwalk. He rubbed his hand across his lips, making sure he had gotten any remains of breakfast off his face. He smiled as he turned and started to walk toward the general store.

As he approached, he looked through the front window and an even bigger smile crossed his face. Betsy was sweeping the items on a shelf with a large feather duster. Just the sight of her made the day seem warmer.

As he reached the door, he was distracted by a grubby man with stringy hair and a beard that surely hadn't been trimmed in years. He might have been distracted by the movement of this unkempt soul, but if the wind was from the other direction, he could have smiled at him long before he had gotten into sight.

"Marshal, take me to the lock up," came from the mouth of the man. His eyes were bloodshot and the utterance had escaped through a row of missing, yellowed teeth.

Kennedy turned to him. "Jonas, I know you're drunk. In fact, you're always drunk, but I don't have the time or see the need to lock you up."

"I'm hungry, and I can get some vittles there."

"Let's talk about that. I lock you up about three times a week, and I know that is about the only place you get anything to eat. All your money goes for drink and since you have no money to pay your fines, you're tearing my budget to pieces. On top of that, I have to wash the place down just to get rid of the smell."

Kennedy reached into his pocket and pulled out the two biscuits. He handed them to Jonas. "You take these and be happy. That's all I can do for you right now. Try to sober up. You might find it somewhat pleasant. If you can't get that done, at least go to the creek and wash yourself. Man, you alone could give this town a bad name."

Kennedy turned to enter the store and a lady with a small girl was headed out. He pushed open the door and stepped to the side. "Good morning, Mrs. Walker, and how are you and that little beauty doing today?"

The lady smiled and the little girl's eyes got bigger as she threw back her head and looked up at the marshal. "Thank you, Marshal. We're doin' fine." She hesitated and an even bigger knowing smile came across her face. "It sure ain't no surprise me a-seein' ya here."

Kennedy smiled back. "You're right. I got to drop by

ever' morning to see that lady in there, and the thing that excites me most is that soon I won't have to be dropping by, but she'll be the first thing I see in the morning."

"Well, the whole town is a-waitin' for that big day."

"Not near as much as me."

They both laughed as she pulled the little girl close to her side and placed her hands over the girl's ears.

"I saw you talkin' to that Jonas feller. Marshal, me and lots of the ladies that's got kids is worried about him. Ever since he came to town, he not only stinks up the place, but he's always talkin' to the walls or the trees or 'bout anything that ya know ain't gonna be answerin' ya back. His eyes is always shiftin' and he gets those hands a-movin' like he expects an answer."

"Mrs. Walker, I know what you're saying, but he is just simple, and on top of that, a drunk. He may stink up the town, and I know his strange actions bother folks, but I'm sure he is harmless. However, if it makes you and the others feel better, I'll keep my eye on him. If any of you see him do anything not right, let me know and I'll try to do something about it."

She stood for a minute and looked him directly in the eye. After a few seconds she nodded. "I'll tell the others, and we is gonna hold ya to that."

She passed on out the door, and he turned toward Betsy.

Betsy dropped the feather duster to her side and walked toward Kennedy. She smiled as she said, "Did you come by for your morning sugar?"

He reached out and put his arm around her waist. "No, don't need that. I stopped at the café and had a good dab of honey with my biscuit."

Betsy rapped the feather duster on his leg. "You devil, you," she said with a light-hearted chuckle. She reached up and kissed him on the cheek. "Now you've got a double dose."

He pulled her around square to him and kissed her on the lips. "I promise you it won't be long 'til we don't have to meet like this."

She smiled and laid her head on his massive shoulder. "Won't be soon enough for me."

"I think—"

He was interrupted by a boy of about sixteen slamming the door behind him. "Marshal, ya told me to tell ya if I ever saw that bunch of rowdies again, and they are back. They're down at the Blue Moon, and when I walked by, they was makin' one hell of a lot of noise."

Kennedy pushed Betsy back slightly. "Hon, I have to go. I'll see you a little later."

She put her hand to her lips and blew him a kiss. "You take care."

CHAPTER TWO

Marshal Kennedy walked into the local saloon with complete confidence. He pushed open the establishment's swinging doors without a second thought. After all, why should he hesitate? He was the marshal of Angel, Texas, he was young, and he had proven himself many times before. The small town was one of several under his watch, and he would not shrink from his duty. He never had before, and now would be no different.

He was the youngest marshal in just about any territory. He had cut his teeth taking down several notorious outlaws when he was just a sheriff. Timmy Bateman, notorious horse thief and murderer, and William Oakley, bank robber, were the more notable ones, but there were many more lawbreakers who Kennedy had put away, some permanently. Unlike a great many other lawmen, he did not have a history of being on the other side of the law before becoming an enforcer. It seemed as if being a lawman was second nature to the young sheriff, and he handled himself magnificently.

The young marshal had more than his share of conquests of the fairer sex. The ladies simply fawned over the handsome and capable lawman who was just a shade under thirty, with his best years in front of him. The local girl who had worked her way to the top of the list (as well as into his heart) was Betsy Ryley. She was the owner of the general store. Her smart and energetic manner coupled with those deep blue eyes and long flowing black hair had captured Johnny from the first time he had met her. She had it all, and it was just a matter of time until she would be jumping over the broom. He had insisted that only when he had a comfortable bank account would that take place, and with the reward offered for Bill Bundy, it seemed that the day was closer than he had expected.

Kennedy heard the hushed whispers and murmurs of several of the bar's patrons as he entered. He even spotted some of the saloon women smiling at him. Despite the seriousness of the visit, he managed to smile and nod toward the girls.

One of the girls tapped another on the shoulder, who was just coming down the stairs. “It's Marshal Kennedy! He's in our saloon!”

The girl looked across the room. “I'm glad to see him. This bunch of pond scum needs to be gone, and I hope he's here to take those no-accounts to the lock-up.”

Clearly, Kennedy's reputation preceded him. It only made him more confident as he approached the three men at the bar.

Johnny's eyes didn't need to wander far before he spotted Bill Bundy. Bundy was a wanted man in several territories, notorious for just about every offense in the book. The law badly wanted Bundy and didn't care how they got him. Kennedy could drag him to a local judge's office kicking and screaming, or in a pine box.

Bundy was drinking with his associates, Tex Winters and Duke Morrison. Kennedy wasn't too worried about them. Both had a reputation of being drunks who could not shoot straight and most of the time were so far gone they couldn't remember which hip their pistol was on.

Johnny took a deep breath and quickly glanced around the room. He did not want to be blind-sided by another member of Bundy's bunch. He had faced that problem before, and his near death had taught him to make sure the man he was after was the only one he needed to focus on.

He stepped to the end of the bar and pulled back his vest, exposing his badge. "All right. Let's get this over with, Bundy. I've got places to go and things to do," Kennedy said.

Bundy turned around and faced the marshal. His eyes were fixed and his jaw muscles tightened. There was not a single trace of fear in his face. He dropped his right hand to his side. "Marshal John Kennedy, I assume. I've heard rumours that you were one tough hombre, but me and my buddies were needing a drink and decided to pay your fair town a visit. We weren't expectin' company. To what do I owe the pleasure?"

Bundy's remark was dripping with sarcasm. His breath was oozing with alcohol, and he even displayed a slight sway as he removed his foot from the foot rest at the bottom on the bar. Other men would have been intimidated by the mere sight of Kennedy, but Bundy treated him like an annoyance.

Kennedy answered with just as much nonchalance. “You know why I'm here, Bundy. I’ve got a stack of papers on you a foot thick, and I need to get you comfortable in a cell so that the judge can decide what to do with you. Now, how about you coming with me, and we get this over with?”

Bundy smiled at Kennedy, revealing several missing teeth. He craned his neck and spit a black wad of tobacco at the spittoon, missing it by several inches. What few chompers he had were stained yellow or black from the tobacco.

“Yeah, let's do that, Marshal. How about we dance?”

Kennedy shook his head. “Tsk, tsk. I warned you, Bundy. I don't want to have to resort to no violence to take you in. And you don’t seem to be my type.”

Kennedy kept his hands close to his holstered guns. He did not take his eyes off Bundy or his friends. Like a watchful hawk, Kennedy was ready for anything now. He had to be. With that one remark, Bundy had thrown down the gauntlet, and Kennedy knew that anything could happen.

Morrison and Winters stumbled back, almost tripping over themselves. It was no surprise that they were drunk, so Kennedy ignored them. The last time he had tangled with them, he had pistol whipped both before they could clear leather. He was sure they would be no threat. If it was necessary, they would be easy to take down, once he had dealt with Bundy.

Bundy glanced at the drunks as they passed by and then took a deep breath as he dropped his shoulders. His hands swung close to his guns.

The previous chatter from surrounding tables died completely and the sound of chairs scooting across the hardwood floor signaled the approach of hostility.

Bundy’s ugly teeth appeared as his lips parted. “Yeah, well, I don't mind resorting to violence. In fact, it kinda makes my day.”

Kennedy knew that Bundy was going to draw his guns. He had a reputation of having an itchy trigger finger. He had shot it out with the law before and was suspected of gunning down several people in his robberies.

Kennedy held his ground. The young lawman was absolutely confident of his own abilities. He had proven himself countless times. There was no doubt that Bundy was dangerous, but Kennedy knew he had taken down worse. There was only one thing he failed to know. Bundy was at his best while he was drunk. There was something about being inebriated that heightened Bundy's senses. The outlaw never hesitated getting intoxicated before any kind of skirmish, and he had the round table muscle hanging over his belt, showing he had done it many a time.

Bundy drew his gun faster than Kennedy expected. The revolver leapt out of its holster, while Kennedy’s was just clearing leather.

Kennedy saw the flame leave the end of Bundy's pistol. He heard the explosion, and he was amazed that he could see the stream of smoke that followed the bullet directly toward his chest. He had been kicked in the chest by a cantankerous mule when he was twelve and that had lifted him off the ground and caused him to spend three days moping around the house. This was worse. The pain followed the cracking of his rib, which he could plainly feel, and instantly his body went numb. He looked down and saw his pistol roll from his hand and clatter as it hit the floor. He could feel his legs step back and then fold under his relaxing weight. The last thing he felt was his head striking a chair and the crashing sound as it shattered from the force of the blow.

Suddenly, a warmth like he had never known swept over his body. The room started to spin, but in an inviting way. The spinning room swiftly turned to a tunnel and there was a light at the end that was more warming than the sun and more peaceful than a babbling brook. He felt himself floating up toward the light, and it was the most relaxing experience he had ever encountered.

Abruptly, his ascent stopped, and he felt as if he was being transported over lands he had ridden on horseback, but now was looking down on them.

Bundy stood over the lawman's corpse. The other patrons of the saloon could only watch in shock and awe. It was an awful sight, no doubt about it, but Bundy beamed in pride at his handiwork. The smell of gunpowder drifted across the room as Bundy turned toward the customers. His pistol was at his side and smoke was rising from the barrel. “Heh. That was easy. Any of ya gents have a problem with what ya just seen?”

These words pulled Kennedy back to the scene inside the saloon. He was totally confused.

CHAPTER THREE

Kennedy opened his eyes. It was almost as if he were waking from a dream.

He shouted, "What happened?" But not a soul acknowledged him. He rolled to his feet and stood, but when he looked around the room not one person looked at him. He looked down and saw his body lying on the floor with his pistol beside him and the splintered chair scattered by his side.

Kennedy reached down and touched his own body. His hand simply sunk into the corpse. He immediately stood up straight and took a step backward. He was confused and disoriented. His consciousness had not fully processed what had just happened. That was understandable, considering that he had just died.

Kennedy took another glance around his surroundings. He saw Bundy smiling in front of him. He saw him spit on the floor. His two drinking companions walked to his side, never taking their eyes off the body lying at the end of the bar.

Bundy pushed the pistol to the brim of his hat and smiled.

The marshal snarled, "What're you smilin' at, Bundy? I'll wipe that smile off your face!" Kennedy pulled out his other pistol. He pulled the trigger. It was all second nature to him, and he could not miss a shot this close, but there was no flame or explosion, no recoil, no anything. He blurted out, "What the hell?"

Kennedy assumed that his gun jammed. It must have. The gun had never jammed before, but it was the only explanation.

Kennedy moved quickly. He still believed he was in a life-and-death struggle, and he swung hard at Bundy with his pistol still at hand. The swing was fast and powerful and should have knocked Bundy senseless. It did not. Instead, his hand seemed to pass right through Bundy. Bundy didn't even acknowledge his presence or the blow that he had so carefully placed. It was almost as if the outlaw didn't even know he was there. Kennedy's eyes grew wide with shock and surprise. His mind was racing, trying to make sense of all of this. He simply couldn't understand what was happening.

Kennedy tried to grab his killer and turn him to face him. His hands melted through his killer's body. "What in tarnation's going on? I'm talking to you, Bundy!"

Winters said, "Ya did a hell of a job there, boss."

Morrison shook his head. "I didn't think ya could do it. I've seen that one in action, and I just didn't think ya could do it. The last time me and Winters seen him, he bounced one of them pistols off our heads and we woke up in jail. When ya told us ya wanted to come to town to get a drink, we was feared ya'd bit off more than ya could chew. But ya sure showed 'im who was boss of this town."

Morrison smiled as he approached Kennedy's corpse

cautiously. He stumbled as he stooped over to pick up Kennedy's pistol. He had to grab the table to get his balance. Winters walked to him and grabbed his arm. The two turned toward Bundy.

Bundy's eyes narrowed. "You bunch of dunderheads, ya act like he's still alive. For your information it's safe now, boys. Kennedy's dead, dead, and dead. I did all the work, of course."

Bundy slapped Winters and Morrison on the backs of their heads. He shook his own.

"Where in hell did I pick ya two up? I'da done better if I'da brought that mule in that the old prospector was a leadin' when I shot 'im."

Kennedy saw and heard all of this, and he still couldn't believe any of it.

"Dead? I'm dead? What the hell are you talking about, Bundy? I'm right here!"

Kennedy took a few more swings at Bundy, and some at Winters and Morrison. The same thing happened. The three men simply ignored him, and his blows went right through them. Perhaps it would be wrong to say that they ignored him. After all, to ignore someone or something, you would have to know it was even there in the first place. No one in that saloon knew that Kennedy's spirit was still there, kicking, tussling and trying to respond. He was like the breeze now, a force that was just there, floating and hovering, unseen.

Kennedy would not give in to the situation. He felt that if he could see them, there must be some way of contacting them. “Winters! Morrison! Bundy! I'm right here! Face me!”

The three men turned their backs on the ranting spirit and nonchalantly ordered more drinks. The bartender was terrified as he served them up. He glanced up from the bottle as his nervous hand tapped the neck on Bundy’s glass. “You, you killed him!”

“Sure did. Maybe you good folks of Angel will take that as a warning. I ain’t puttin’ up with no disrespect.”

Bundy turned around as Jack Jameson, a resident of Angel, entered. He had been one of Kennedy’s biggest supporters. Kennedy remembered Jack as a decent sort of fellow who never caused any trouble. He remembered meeting Jack in his early days as the sheriff of Angel. He could still recollect how nervous Jack was. Jack was a young man who thought the world of Kennedy. It never really mattered to the marshal until now.

Kennedy's mind brought him back to that first moment that he met Jack. He had not really even thought about Jack until this awful moment.

Kennedy remembered the excitement in the young man’s voice as he had stuck out his hand. “You're... you're Jack Kennedy! I've heard all about you, mister! I know all about how you took down that crazy killer Jim Walton and his gang!”

Jameson was trembling in front of Kennedy, while

Kennedy was sitting behind his table, clearly bored.

He finally looked up and extended his hand. "Yeah, that's me. I did all that, but don't believe everything you read in those dime novels. Believe me, kid, a gunfight's a lot more dangerous in real life than in the written word. When you do it on paper, you can erase the mistakes. Face-to-face, it is what it is."

The irony of the memory could not escape Kennedy, for he knew if only he had listened to his own advice, he would not be in this strange setting.

Kennedy had downplayed the young man's hero worship, but Jack Jameson would not be deterred. "I'm here to apply for that deputy position you got."

"That so? Sure, kid. You got any experience in gunfights, fighting for your life, and that sort of thing?"

Jameson hesitated before answering. He shook his head. "Not really, Mister Kennedy. But hey, I can learn!"

The boy's cheekiness was oozing out of his body. Jameson was clearly a greenhorn, but it was obvious that he was filled with enthusiasm and wanted to join in the marshal's efforts. Kennedy had to give him a chance.

"I won't let you down if you take me in sir, and—"

Kennedy raised up a hand. "Yep. I got it. Son, before I take you in, I want to see what you can do."

A smile engulfed Jameson's face as he wiped his hands on the front of his pants. "Yessir, all right, sir!"

Kennedy led Jameson out of his office and into a wide field. He pointed in the distance. "You see them tin cans over there?"

Jameson's eyes travelled in the direction Kennedy's finger was pointing. When he squinted his eyes and looked a little closer, he finally spotted them. The cans were right in front of him, just some distance away. They were pretty small, and that was why it was hard to spot them at first. But yeah, they were there, all right.

"I see 'em, Marshal!"

"Good. Take one of these."

Kennedy handed Jackson his revolver. Jameson took it, and he noticed how heavy it was. He grabbed the barrel with his left hand and pulled the weapon to his body. He looked up at the marshal and forced a knowing smile on his face.

"That there's a Colt. It's one of the most reliable pistols a man of my trade can have. It's got great stopping power and reasonable range. Them cans are small, and a good distance away, but they can be hit with it. Try 'n' shoot 'em."

It was a reasonable request. Most men were expected to handle a firearm with at least some degree of competence, and most could; but it was obvious, just from his mannerisms, that Jameson had little or no experience with a firearm and the only thing he had going for him were the "want-to-dos" of life.

"Yes, sir. Shoot 'em, I will!"

Kennedy could see that the young Jameson was nervous, and he didn't expect him to hit the cans. They were pretty far off. Still, maybe there was something there that he could work with.

Jameson fired several shots. Kennedy could already see that none of them hit the mark. There was dirt flying from in front of the target to behind the target. A limb from a tree three feet from the cans broke and hung half suspended after one shot. Nothing that looked or sounded like the shooter had even come close to what he was supposed to be hitting could be observed.

With the explosion of the sixth round, Kennedy held up his hand. "Wait here. I'll get them cans." Kennedy gathered the cans and returned to Jameson. He showed them to him. "Well, as you can see, you didn't hit a single one."

"I can hit 'em! I can hit 'em! Just gimme a chance!"

Kennedy raised a hand with his palm toward Jameson. The kid was clearly ready and raring to go. He had enthusiasm—that much was certain. "Yeah, take it easy. I'll place 'em on those tree stumps over there. That'll be a lot closer for you. You should be able to hit at least one of 'em."

Jameson turned toward the stumps. A hopeful smile appeared as he pulled the pistol to his chest. He shook his head and took a deep breath as his eyes narrowed, watching Kennedy place the cans.

Kennedy placed the cans on the tree stumps. He had thought as he walked back that this was a much more reasonable distance.

"Okay, kid. Try shooting at the cans now."

"I can do this! I can shoot 'em! I'll be yer deputy, an' they can make dime novels about me! I'll be famous-like!"

"Shut yer trap an' let 'er rip, already!"

Jameson lifted the pistol and worked hard to make sure it was steady. He pulled the trigger and... *click*.

Kennedy broke into a hard laugh. "I'd guess that's one of the first things you have got to learn. My boy, you can't fire a pistol if it isn't loaded, and you'd be better off with a Bowie knife than a pistol if it isn't loaded." Pulling cartridges from his belt, he handed the boy six rounds. "See if you can pass that test."

There was nothing smooth are relaxed about the loading process, but Jameson finally snapped the cylinder shut and looked up at Kennedy with a relieved smile on his face.

The marshal pointed at the stump. "Have your go."

Jameson obliged and fired at the cans. They should have been easy shots for a man with any kind of experience, but Jameson missed them all.

Kennedy didn't need to look to see that Jameson had missed the marks completely. It was a disappointment for Kennedy, but it was heart-breaking for Jameson.

Kennedy approached Jameson, and his look said it all. "Uh… okay, kid. You didn't hit a single one. I don't think that—"

"Come on, Marshal Kennedy! Give me another chance! I know I can be a great deputy for ya!"

Kennedy shook his head. "Nope. Sorry, kid, but my line of work's dangerous. A lot more dangerous than you think and—"

"Please, Marshal! I know I can be a great deputy if you give me a chance."

Kennedy was adamant. He reached for his revolver that Jameson was holding tightly in his hand. It was apparent that he wanted to resist, but he meekly surrendered it.

"Hey, swing and a miss, eh? Sorry, kid. Them's the breaks. I need someone who can shoot straight, no offense."

Jameson knew that his chance was over, and he bowed his head. "You're going to regret this, Marshal. You do know that, don't 'cha? I may not be a straight shot, but I'm pretty dependable. The next hombre you get may not be so."

"I know that, Jack. I really do. Sorry."

About a week after Jameson's job interview, another candidate for the position of deputy waltzed into Kennedy's office. Rory Bowman—he shot all of those cans without a second thought. After only a few weeks though, he was fired for excessive drinking. When Kennedy walked into the saloon, he was still in the middle of looking for a deputy. Now that he was dead, he was starting to wonder if he should have hired Jack.

Jack walked toward the marshal's lifeless body, still on the saloon floor. "You killed the marshal, you damn worthless weasel!"

Bundy looked down on Jack. He was crouched near Kennedy's corpse.

"I've a mind to have you join the good marshal in eternity, young 'un. However, I'm not going to do that. Not now, at least. Yer not worth the effort, or the extra bullet. So's I would advise that ya make the most of this little pass I'm givin' and make yerself scarce."

Jameson glared at Bundy as he rose. He kept his eyes on Bundy as he worked his way to the door. The toe of his boot caught on the leg of a chair and sent it clattering across the room. Bundy broke out in laughter as Jameson stumbled through the door.

Winters and Morrison snickered, but looked back from the swinging door and expressed their concern.

Winters said, “The kid looked real mad, boss.”

Morrison stroked his chin and said, “Looked like he won’t take the marshal’s death lying down. You ask me, he's going to cause some trouble in one form or another. Makes me a little antsy.”

Bundy slapped Morrison on the back hard. Morrison almost spit up his liquor.

“Just about everything gets you antsy, Duke! Yer a regular pussycat! I don't know why I even keep you in this little outfit of mine!”

“Because you like me?”

“Maybe because I need someone to make me laugh now and then. Close enough!”

“I'll take that as a compliment, boss...”

“Take it any way you like! It don't matter how you take it, just like it don't matter what that kid’s going to do! He ain't going to be much trouble. I'll just call in the other boys, and this town’ll be ours!”

Kennedy didn't like what he was hearing. “The other boys” were other outlaws in Bundy’s gang. Outlaws that were a lot more intimidating than Winters and Morrison. Those boys were bad news and could easily cause a lot more trouble than the other two.

It was bad news for Angel, for sure. The town would

be sacked by those outlaws, and nothing good would come of it. But what could the late Marshal John Kennedy do? He was no good for anyone now. He was dead. The dead couldn't do anything but stay dead. Or could they?

CHAPTER FOUR

So, I'm dead now. So this is what it's like to be deader than a rock. It sure wasn't what I expected it to be...

Marshal Johnny expected death to be different. All men do, and truth be told, when the hour is finally there, death is often quite different for each one.

He had been raised with the usual expectations of how one would pass from this world to the next. He often thought that he would see the bright light and his spirit would be led there, to some grand paradise or whatever else awaited him. If not a bright light, perhaps death would be eternal slumber, as the ancient Greek philosophers often intoned. Nothing but a blackness where there would be no consciousness, and you could feel neither pain, suffering, nor joy or hope. Nothing but the comfort of the eternal abyss and a complete extinguishing of the consciousness. Neither happened to poor John Kennedy when he passed on. He was pulled back from the light, and there wasn't any of the nothingness that would completely engulf a once live spirit. None of that sort happened, and instead, death seemed to be something much worse than life.

The marshal's spirit merely wandered on in Angel, and he was forced to watch as Bundy and his gang visited unspeakable horrors upon the town he was sworn to protect.

Marshal Kennedy could do nothing as Bill Bundy and his boys sacked and pillaged the town. He watched helplessly as the outlaws gorged themselves on death and chaos. It was a terrible fate for Angel, and Kennedy wished he could somehow stop them, or at least keep himself from seeing it all play out. He could do neither.

"Help! Someone help me!"

Kennedy watched in horror as Betsy cried for help. There was no one who could answer her. Everyone else was too busy trying to stay alive as Bundy and his boys wreaked their destruction.

"Betsy!" Kennedy cried out and reached for Betsy. It was completely futile. She couldn't hear or see him. No one could.

"Come here, baby!"

It was Bundy. He grabbed Betsy just as she ran out of the hardware store. She had barely managed to get out in time, as the whole place was burning. The flames were huge. They were popping and cracking as sparks and flames twisted and turned while reaching for the heavens.

Betsy and her late parents had invested everything they had in that general store. It had been built with blood, sweat, and tears literally. When they had passed on, they left the store in Betsy's care. She took the responsibility very seriously. That was until this terrible moment. Now, it was burning to the ground in front of her eyes. Bill Bundy had her locked tightly in his arms, and he was not letting go. His free hand was exploring her body like she was some cheap dance hall girl.

"Someone help me, please!"

"Heh. Ain't no one going to help you, baby. The whole town's too busy cowering in fear!"

Kennedy wanted to turn away. This was all getting too hard to watch. The outlaws fired their guns in the air, and the townspeople simply scampered away, or ran back into their homes. The most important store in Angel was burning, and Betsy was being ravaged by Bundy. It was all happening in front of them, and there was nothing they could do. They were simply too afraid.

Let go of her, you monster! Kennedy wailed and screamed at Bundy, but it was useless. No one even knew he was there. He could not affect the outcome of these terrible events in any way. *You God damn pig! Don't you have any kind of decency in your system? Stop this!*

Kennedy could have been howling at the wind. He could do nothing as Bundy carried out his dastardly act to its end. When he finished ravaging her, he pulled up his pants and walked away. Betsy was left in the middle of the road, sobbing helplessly. She was clearly broken and shattered, beyond any kind of repair.

"Hah! That'll show you! That'll show all of you good people of Angel! Betsy here wasn't willing to pay us the protection fee that we asked for! It wasn't much, considering all this could have been avoided if she'd just paid up!"

More gunfire accompanied Bundy's rants. No one in the town dared answer back.

"Consider this a warning—an example, if you will—of what will happen if any of you don't give in to me and my boys' reasonable demands! The law is dead in Angel! We're the new law around here now!"

It was all a sight that Kennedy could not bear. It was too much to bear for any living man, but having passed on, it only seemed to infuriate Kennedy even more. Death was supposed to be a repose from such terrible things.

Now, it seemed as if fate were playing a cruel joke on him, as he was forced to see his town and the people in it suffering. They were suffering, and there was nothing he could do.

Make it stop! Make it stop! I can't bear to see any of this anymore!

The marshal was pleading with fate itself to do anything to stop the injustices around him. He would receive no satisfactory answer. What he would get, would be even more pain and misery.

The shot rang out from out of nowhere. The bullet whizzed past Bundy, taking off his hat. He ducked in response and his horse bolted at the same time. Bundy struggled to keep in the saddle, but gravity outdid his effort and he toppled to the ground.

He scrambled to his knees and turned in the direction of the shot. The shot had startled everyone, even Kennedy. Nearly every person in the street turned to see who had fired the shot.

It was Jack Jameson. His trembling hands were holding a rifle. He was shaking so hard it was visible.

Jack, you fool, what have you done?

Kennedy cursed the young man's inability to shoot straight. He cursed that he had not taken the time to teach the willing young man at least how to extinguish a polecat.

"Get that varmint! He tried to kill me!" Bundy screamed.

Bundy pointed at Jack as he knelt on the ground. His men responded immediately and rode towards him. Jack managed to fire a few more rounds, but none of them hit any of the outlaws. They had all seen just how inept he was with the rifle, and it only emboldened them. One of the outlaws fired at Jameson. He went down as he felt the bullet pierce his side.

Once on the ground, the outlaws swarmed all over Jameson like ants on a piece of sweet cake. Jameson raised his rifle to fire, but it was impossible. One of the outlaws descended from his horse and landed a brutal fist to Jameson's face.

"Yee-haw! You're dead now, boy!"

"Beat him up! Everyone beat him up!"

Jameson dropped the rifle, and they all descended upon him. They began to beat him mercilessly. Blow upon blow fell upon him. He was totally defenceless.

Stop! Stop it already! You're killing him! Kennedy watched in horror as the outlaws beat Jameson. It was not enough that they had sacked the town, burned the store, and violated Betsy. It seemed as if Bundy's appetite for destruction knew no limits.

"Stop!"

The outlaws turned and saw Bundy. He moved towards them with his hand up. They would have beaten Jameson to death, if he had not stopped them.

"That's enough!"

Bundy stopped them from killing Jameson outright, but Kennedy knew that it was not out of mercy. Someone like Bundy had none of it in his heart.

"Boss? We ain't killin' him?"

"Do you really have to make it a habit to annoy me, Morrison? Do I always have to explain myself to you?"

"I don't understand, boss…"

"You never do! Nobody kill him! He shot at me, an' I want to be the one to personally do it. Let's hang 'im high! And let me be the one to personally string him up! I want to have that satisfaction."

Kennedy turned away as the outlaws grabbed Jameson and marched him to his grim fate. He could not take any of this any longer.

Dear God, is this what death is like? Am I cursed to forever just idly watch as injustices occurs? I used to be a lawman, and a damn good one at that. Must I be punished for eternity for a moment of miscalculation? Isn't there a way to stop all of this? This is a fate worse than death!

The spirit cried and pleaded in anguish, but no one heard him. The outlaws took Jameson away to face his fate at the hanging tree, and there was nothing Kennedy could do about it.

CHAPTER FIVE

Bundy pushed Jameson under the tree. The three men who had walked with them grabbed an arm or a leg and held Jack still as Bundy put the loop over his head. He was so beaten up that there was no need for that much physical restraint.

"Get that up over that limb. I want to see this here so-called brave man danglin', and I want the town to see it, so they know what might come their way if they didn't get enough learnin' from the store fire. In fact, some of ya go round up a few, so we make sure that they enjoy what's a-comin' to someone that tries to stand in the way of our fun."

Bundy pulled the rope and lifted Jack off the ground. He held him there for a moment and then let his feet return to the ground.

"Ain't that fun?" Now ya got a little taste of what's awaitin' ya."

Happy now, boy? You think you're gonna be some great gunslinger, gunning down desperadoes while they make dime novels about you? Are you happy? Tell me. Kennedy watched the action and wanted to move. Where was his knife and why couldn't he use it?

Bundy pulled on the rope. It was already tight and Jack Jameson's body twisted and turned as he struggled for one last breath of air.

Jack's lips moved but his eyes closed. Saliva drooled from his mouth. His legs continued to flail.

"Yeah! Go ahead an' squirm, kid! I got all the time in the world to see you die. Your town's mine now. If you were smarter, you would have just accepted that fact, instead-a trying to play hero!"

A sudden clap of thunder shook the ground and a bolt of lightning lit up the area. Instantly a deluge of rain fell, pelting the onlookers. The glow from the lightning outlined Jack as he hung from the tree. The rain pounded hard. It was as if the very heavens were protesting the horrible acts of Bundy and his gang.

"Rain came outta nowhere! We're gonna get soaked! Let's leave him, boss!" Morrison said. When he turned to Bundy, a stream of water ran off the bill of his hat.

"You go ahead an' leave, Morrison. You were always a little girl in these matters. Afraid of ghosts, goblins, an' gettin' wet and contracting something! You're a real little yellowbelly!"

The outlaws all laughed as Bundy belittled Morrison. That was when lightning crackled and sparkled all around them. A lightning bolt cut through the air, illuminating everything for a moment. The sudden flash of light was followed by the booming sound of thunder. The light and sound display was like nothing any had ever seen. The bolts were so numerous that it was like a gunfight, but the force of the display rattled the onlooker's nerves. The ground quaked and the barn next to the tree shuddered.

"Whoa! That was something else! It's a lightning storm!"

The group looked from one to the other as they turned up their collars or pulled down their hats. All were soaked—their clothes stuck to their bodies and rainwater ran from their hats. The rain fell so fast and in such a great amount that it made a hissing sound. The gang ran into the barn for their horses. A few splashed through the puddles as they ran back toward the cover of the porch attached to the saloon. The group suddenly looked like they were in a total state of panic, except for Bundy. He remained rooted to the ground and did not even flinch, although his hat and clothes were soaked and he blinked as the rain hit him in his uplifted face. He held onto the rope with firm hands and was not the least bit startled.

"All you boys want to get out, that's fine by me. I'm stayin' here, like Ben Franklin! A little rain an' lights never hurt nobody. Besides, I want to see this fool squirm before he dies."

With those words, the few who had stayed rushed to their horses and rode off. Bundy was left behind with Jameson.

"Looks like it's just you an' me, hero."

Bundy's voice was dripping with contempt. He genuinely hated Jameson for taking a stand against him, and he wanted him to suffer.

“I'm the only one here. I’m the last thing you're going to see before you go into the great beyond. I sure hope that it was worth it!”

Bundy was nothing but a petty and sadistic man. He knew nothing but lawlessness and delighted in seeing others suffer as long as it suited him.

Jameson expired in the hangman’s noose as the rain fell. The thunder and lightning protested one more time the death of a good man. Bundy never did flinch. The outlaw was rotten at the core.

Bundy looked up and saw that Jameson was not squirming on the rope anymore. His body was simply hanging limply and motionless. Bundy smiled when he realized that Jack was definitely dead.

“Ain’t movin’ no more, eh? Yeah. You're dead an’ you deserve it.”

He let the rope slip from his hands and Jack’s lifeless body fell to the muddy ground with a squelch. Without a moment’s hesitation, Bundy began walking away. It seemed that he had no remorse for having hanged an idealistic and decent young man. After he got about halfway to the saloon, he broke into a trot, finally getting annoyed with the rain.

Jack Jameson died hanging from a tree that dark and stormy night. He died, and the spirit of Marshal John Kennedy was not there to witness it.

CHAPTER SIX

It took all his will to do it, but Kennedy managed to get himself out of Angel. It was a strange sensation, one of many that was now assaulting the dead lawman. For a moment, it seemed as if he were rooted to Angel. It was almost as if he were pulled there, as if the town was exerting some kind of magnetic force on Kennedy.

It was inexplicable, but it was what he felt. Kennedy felt drawn to the town, drawn to witness all the horrors that were happening. For a moment, he thought he might never ever be able to leave, but suddenly, during the midst of that lightning storm as he was watching Jack Jameson's demise, he was gone.

Now, Kennedy was somewhere else. Someplace different.

I thought I would never get out of that town. I thought I would be cursed to see all that pain and suffering forever. Now, I'm... I'm just not there anymore. What's going on?

Kennedy looked around and saw that he was in a bleak place. There were no outlaws here, only parched and infertile land. The land was dotted with a few makeshift structures where a few emaciated people moved about. Men, women and children were thin, and it looked as if it had been months since they had eaten. They looked more ghost-like than Kennedy, and their desperation was written on their faces. Kennedy immediately recognized the place. The bleakness and the desperation around him was evidence enough of where it was. He immediately recognized the sadness of the people around him.

The Indian reservation...

A deep voice came out of nowhere, "So, the spirit of the white man finally arrives."

Kennedy turned around. He saw an Indian sitting on the ground. He looked quite old and had a bottle of whiskey beside him. His legs were crossed and the buffalo hide he sat on looked as if it had seen better days. The old man looked a little drunk but seemed calm and at peace. He did not look as desperate as the others. His braids hung to the middle of his chest and they were streaked with gray.

"Greetings, white spirit."

Kennedy looked at the old Indian with amazement. "You can... you can see and hear me? Even if I'm dead?"

The old Indian's lips curled into a smile. "You find that surprising? Yes, I can sense your presence, while others cannot. I can communicate with you. I did send for you here. I had sent for you once before, but decided that you needed to see what was going to happen to those you were supposed to protect."

Kennedy's eyes grew wide with surprise. "So that was what that flying through the land was all about."

The Indian nodded. Kennedy slowly walked toward the man. "This is all quite unbelievable and hard to process."

"You have task ahead of you."

"Whoa, whoa. Slow down here, old timer. I just died. It's a bit of a... shock."

The Indian nodded as he took a swig of whiskey. "Understandable. What do you need to know?"

"A lot of things! First of all, how did you summon me? You're telling me you've got power over me?"

"Some power, yes. If you noticed earlier, you probably could not leave Angel, could you? You witnessed your town being ravaged by Bill Bundy and his gang of misfits. You were frustrated by your inability to influence any of the events that had transpired. You wanted to leave and spare yourself the agony of being a silent witness. But you could not. Like a moth to a flame, your spirit seemed to be drawn to Angel and its suffering. You wished with all your heart you could leave that place, and finally, you did. And worst yet, you shuddered and struggled while the one you love was violated. You wanted to turn away but found you couldn't. Now, you're here."

"That's exactly how it happened, old timer. I'm impressed. You're legit, all right, and you've got my attention. I guess you probably know that I'm Marshal—"

"John Kennedy, yes. I know who you are. I am Spirit Speaker. I am my tribe's shaman."

"Spirit Speaker, eh? So you can summon spirits and speak to them?"

"Exactly. It is a talent that has been passed on in my family for generations. My father was the tribe's shaman, as was his before him. I am merely fulfilling my duty and carrying on their legacy."

"If you can summon and speak to spirits, are you telling me that you called my spirit from my body?"

Spirit Speaker nodded. "That is exactly what I did."

Upon hearing Spirit Speaker's words, a great rage burned in Kennedy. If he could strangle the old man now, he would. "You no good, son of a—"

Spirit Speaker raised a hand. "Please. No need for profanity here. After all, you're dead." The old Indian took another swig of the whiskey and laughed.

Kennedy was infuriated. "Are you mocking me? Do you think this is funny? You summoned me! My spirit could have moved on, couldn't it? When I died, I could have just known peace, but you summoned me! You're the reason why I have to see so much suffering, while being powerless to stop it. It's torture! If you think that's funny well, you're a sick old man, who's had way too much to drink. Why would you deny me that peace? Why would you subject me to this? I didn't even know you until now!"

Spirit Speaker raised a finger at Kennedy. Suddenly, it seemed as if a tornado's winds had changed direction, and the old man's mood changed drastically. His amusement was gone, and now he too, was angry.

"Do not dare to judge me, white spirit! Not after everything you and your kind have done to my people! Look around you. Look at this place. We once roamed the entire land, free to do as we pleased! Now, we live here in these settlements where you toss us away. The land is small, and we live cramped with little to eat. We cannot farm because of the parched land, and your government promises aid. Aid that never comes.

"We were the first in these lands, but you and your kind took all that away. You used your forked tongues to deceive us with wrongful trade. You tricked us with empty promises. If that did not work, you used the power of the gun to have your way. You feel the pain of your town under the sway of Bundy, do you not? I have seen that kind of pain multiplied a thousand fold. You once called yourself a lawman, did you not? Well, where is the law, where is the justice the law of nature should be here among my people, but instead the law of the white eyes has placed a curse on my people?"

Kennedy was stunned to silence. The old Indian definitely had a point. He had just not seen any of it while he was alive. Perhaps, he refused to see it.

"I... I'm sorry, Spirit Speaker. I did not know. I guess I was blind to it. To all of it."

"You all are."

"I'm truly sorry, Spirit Speaker, but I still need to know why you would summon me?"

"Because of all of this. My people are in need. They are suffering. I am their medicine man. I too have been corrupted. I've done nothing but drink away the pain with the fire liquid your people sent to us as a curse. No, I cannot keep closing my eyes to such things. I sent for you because you can right these wrongs. You can help my people, and others who are in need. You were a good man when you were alive. A lawman who only wanted to see justice done. Death cannot destroy that sense of justice. Not yet."

"I can't help anyone anymore. I can't do any of that. I'm dead!"

The old man took another swig of his whiskey. The whiskey dripped from his mouth as he spoke. "You can do much more than you think. You do not know your true power."

"True power? Have you lost your mind? It must be all that whiskey talking. You seem to know everything about me and what's happening, so surely you know that I can't do anything in this form. I can't touch anyone or anything. I'm nothing but air!"

Spirit Speaker shook his head and dropped his bottle. The hollow thud told him there was no need to try and retrieve it.

"You white men are all the same. Even in death, you know nothing. You have great power. All you need to do is harness it."

"Harness it? How am I going to do that?" He shook his head for a moment, then slowly said, "Can you show me?"

Spirit Speaker smiled at Kennedy. His hands fumbled on the ground for the empty bottle. When he picked it up, he raised it in front of him. "I'll show you for another drink."

CHAPTER SEVEN

Jonas Flannigan had worked hard to be the most disliked man in the town of Angel. A homeless drifter, and with no work, Jonas often lived day by day and hand to mouth. It was a miracle that he even managed to get by, considering his sensitive mental state.

Jonas was the town fool. It was accepted by everyone in Angel that Jonas had mental issues, and no one really knew why. It was simply an accepted fact that he coped by drowning his sorrows in any kind of alcohol he could come by.

Jonas lived in the streets of Angel, drifting around in a drunken haze. He was a man of no consequence, until now. When Bundy and his gang of criminals took over the town, they did not bother to give someone like Jonas a second look. The standing joke among the gang was that one day he would simply drink himself to death, so there was no need in wasting a bullet on him.

What no one counted on was his one gift. His apparent insanity made his mind much more sensitive to other things. Things normal people usually could not see or hear.

Jonas sat in a corner beside the livery stable. He was muttering to himself and his hands seemed to be shooing something—or someone—away. To most people, he was waving at air. Jonas, however, knew better. He could see the spirit of Jack Jameson.

"What are you doing hanging around here with me anyway, Jack? You're just like all the other snobs in town. You never gave a hoot about me when you were alive."

"I'm sorry about that, Jonas. I wish I was nicer to you before, but I can't do anything about that now. I'm just asking you to help me. You're the only one who knows my spirit's still stuck here in Angel. We can't let Bundy and his gang run the town like this!"

Jonas shrugged his shoulders. "We can't? Why not? I don't really care about those folks. Not one kindness did I get from them. They never cared about me, so why should I care about them? If you ask me, life didn't really change much when Bundy took over. Still the same uncaring town, only now it's run by outlaws. And in truth they have not made one difference in my life."

"You don't mean that, Jonas. Bundy's a killer! He killed me and some other townsfolk! I was just the only one that came back."

"And I'm the only one who can see you. I get it, Jack. I know what happened, and I don't care. I just want to finish my drink in peace. Stop pestering me, already!"

Jack was frustrated. His death was slow and agonizing. His hatred for Bundy and his ilk was ever-present, but he could do nothing. All he could do was nag the town fool. He could not stop them in his lifetime, and death only seemed to be one sick joke. It only seemed to provide him with a glimpse of events that he had no control over.

Jack didn't know what else to say to Jonas. He had been hovering around him since his hanging. No one else in the besieged town could see or sense him. Jonas was the only one who could see him, but he did have a point. Even if Jonas was more receptive, what could either of them possibly do against Bundy? In the short time that they were there, he and his men had gained a stranglehold on the town of Angel. What could a restless spirit and the drunk town fool possibly do to stop them?

Jack Jameson pondered the question over and over, but he could find no satisfactory answer. He felt so helpless, and it frustrated him.

"There has to be something we can do! Damn it all, there has to be something!"

Instinctively, Jack lashed out with his anger. His anger was so great that it was palpable now, and he released it all. The unexpected recipient of all of Jack's rage was the bottle in Jonas' hand.

It suddenly shattered into a million pieces, as if Jack had hurled a stone at it.

"Ow! What the hell?"

Jonas instinctively recoiled his hand from the shattered bottle. Both of them looked at it with surprise and disbelief.

"Did, did I just shatter that bottle?"

“You sure did.” Someone had answered Jack’s query, and it was not Jonas.

“Behind you, Jack! Look!”

Jonas pointed behind Jack, and he turned around. Jameson saw a familiar figure.

“Marshal? Marshal Kennedy?”

John Kennedy nodded and smiled at Jack Jameson. He had returned to Angel to find them both. It was exactly as Spirit Speaker had said.

“Hello, Jack. Jonas. I'm back in town.”

The marshal was a lot more confident now than he was before. He did not seem restless or as desperate as Jack was. He seemed a lot more at peace with himself and this whole bizarre situation.

“You’re... you’re a ghost too, Marshal?” Jack said.

The marshal nodded. “Yep. I was already a ghost when that no-account Bundy sacked the town. I saw all of it, and there was nothing I could do.”

Jack’s eyes lit up. “Then you know. You know what I'm going through! That helplessness! That feeling of uselessness in this form!”

“I do, but we’re not useless, Jack. We can stop Bundy once and for all.”

"How is that?"

"I need a body."

"What do you mean by that?"

Kennedy didn't answer. He turned to Jonas. "I need a fighter, Jonas, and you're it."

Jonas' eyes narrowed. "I'm your fighter indeed. That's how I got here. No one ever asked me where I came from or why I was like I am. My brother George and I were in Mosby's Rangers during the war and we was fightin' fools. We killed more men than we could count, and we were terrors with the carbine and shotgun, as well as packin' two six-shooters. We was on raid one late afternoon and we got hit with cannon fire. It blowed poor George up and into little pieces and knocked down me and my horse. When I came to, George was standin' by my side, and I had a huge knot on my head and a headache that woulda killed a bear. George told me it would be all right and that he'd take care of me from them on. So he and I headed west and we ended up here in Angel. George tells me things all the time, and he gets me money and food from time to time. He is my only friend, and no one ever pays me any mind until you guys showed up just like George, 'cause no one can see him either."

Kennedy and Jameson looked at each other. Kennedy said, "That is unreal. It seems that if it wasn't for your injury and the death of your brother, Jameson and I would be in a real fix."

Jameson said, "If a dead man can have luck, it looks like we have it."

Kennedy looked at Jonas. "Sounds like you have the experience, but in your condition, you can't do what needs to be done. Therefore, I'm taking charge of your body."

"You're what?" Jonas' eyes went as wide as saucers.

"My soul and heart and strength are going to enter your body and totally control it. It will be your eyes, your body, and you will actually be there, but I will be doing all the action and talking, if there is any. I promise I'll return all back to you in good shape. But to keep you from panicking, you ask George about it. I hope he has learned in the spirit world what I'm talking about."

Jonas was famous for having blank looks on his face, but this one was the winner of all looks. He slowly turned and walked toward the outhouse. He stopped about five feet from the front door and started talking. His hands were moving from his side to extended in front of him and then to the sides of his head. He dropped them to his hips and shrugged his shoulders.

He returned and said, "Brother George says it will be all right. But he wants you to let him go and watch. He says it's been a long time since he has seen any action and would like to at least see this."

Kennedy smiled. "He is welcome to watch. In fact, if he knows how, he can help."

CHAPTER EIGHT

"Pour me another drink, barkeep."

Hank, the barkeep, reached across the bar and poured whiskey in Bundy's glass. It was the saloon's most expensive brand, but he did not hesitate to serve it to Bundy. The barkeep knew that Bundy would not pay a single cent for any of it, but he didn't complain. There was more than enough reason to complain. The whiskey was expensive, but Bundy and his boys had no qualms about drinking it, or any of his other stock, for free. He was already paying the gang an outrageous fee for protection, and it was all starting to add up. Soon, the stocks would run dry, and he would have no profit to show for it. It would be disastrous, but the barkeep figured that he would simply have to deal with the hand that was dealt him. Despite Bundy and his gang's reprehensible behavior, he did not dare open his mouth. After all, he didn't want to end up like Marshal Kennedy, Jack Jameson, or any of the other men who had dared to stand up to Bundy and his boys. No, the barkeep still wanted to stay alive. He had no intentions of leaving this life in a pine box. Not yet.

It was just another night for Bill Bundy and his boys. A night that was full of drinking and drunken madness, at no cost at all.

Bundy lifted his glass. "This is the life, eh, boys?"

Winters said, "You said it, boss! Having this town to ourselves is just great!"

"I've lost count of all the nights we've gotten drunk here, boss. Ain't no one's standing up to us, and we're the kings of this place!"

"Of course, we're the kings of this place! Anyone that dares stand against us, gets a one way ticket to eternity. What did I tell ya, boys? Stick with me, and we'll all have a great time! All while making a whole lot of money."

Bundy took a gulp of the whiskey and slid his glass towards the barkeep again. "Come on, Hank, old buddy. One more round for me and the boys. All on me!" He let out a malicious laugh.

Bundy's gang all roared their approval as Bundy ordered more drinks.

Hank controlled himself. His face reflected a mixture of fear and anger. He poured the drinks and emptied the bottle. He held it up and looked at the emptiness. He released a sigh as he looked at the pile in the basket under the bar. With an underhand toss, he threw it into the basket. The shattering of the glass seemed to give him some form of relief.

Two empty glasses tapped on the top of the bar. "Hey, old man, ya missed me. Get another bottle so me and my buddy can join the others."

Hank looked from the basket of broken bottles to the shelf. He begrudgingly uncorked a new bottle. "Coming up, Bill."

The swinging doors of the saloon squeaked as they swung open. Bundy and his gang all turned to them, as they weren't used to people entering while they had control of the establishment. A man stepped inside the saloon. He reeked of cheap whiskey and had clearly not bathed in several months. They all immediately recognized him. The only thing that made them hesitate was the outstanding buffalo coat that he had pulled tight to his body.

"You don't need to serve them any more drinks, Hank. It ain't fair that you're serving them, but you always hesitated serving me."

"Jonas Flannigan? You mind taking a bath first before you step into the saloon? You smell like an outhouse!"

Bundy covered his nose, just as the others did. Some of them even chuckled with amusement. It was entertaining to find the town fool suddenly entering the bar.

"I don't need to take no bath, Bundy. As far as I'm concerned, I'm not as dirty as all of you."

Bundy and the others were taken back by Jonas. There was something different about him. He seemed to move and speak with much more confidence. The stutter in his speech was gone, and he stood and walked straight. Usually, he could barely stand, and if he even walked, he would stumble in his drunkenness. Now, he moved purposefully and with no hesitation.

Bundy's eyes narrowed as he glanced from his men back to Jonas. "You really are crazy if you think you can talk to me and my boys like that!"

Jonas nodded and smiled at Bundy. He wiped the buffalo coat sleeve across his face. "Yep. I guess I am."

Before any of them knew what was happening, Jonas threw back the right side of the buffalo coat and whipped out a sawed-off shotgun. When he pulled it out, he moved like the wind, and the gang froze in surprise. They all started dropping their glasses. The scattered shattering mingled with the curses that flowed from the gang. They started reaching for their side arms.

Jonas clasped the stock with his left hand and swung the weapon toward Bundy. Bundy's eyes bulged out as weapon exploded and the charge hit him squarely in the chest. It sent his body flying backward. His mutilated corpse sent a chair crashing across the room. His remains landed in the lap of two of his henchmen. The dead weight tipped over one man's chair. As he grabbed for balance, he ripped the shirt of the man next to him, and they both fell to the floor.

Another member, struggling to get untangled from the mass of bodies, shouted, "He shot the boss! Kill him!"

Normally, the outlaws' retribution would have been swift and deadly. After all, Jonas was the town fool, a drunk simpleton who was not believed to be anything near a fighter, much less a gunslinger. Normally, they would have shot him dead on the spot for what he had done. But this was anything but normal.

Before the outlaws could get organized, all the glasses and bottles of liquor on the wall behind the barkeep exploded. They shattered all at once, as if some giant, unseen hand had slammed against them.

Hank fell forward with the liquor running down his back, glass crashing all around him. In his terror he instinctively ducked under the bar. The glass rang out as it burst, and liquid ran so furiously that it looked similar to the rainfall the night they hung Jameson. The outlaws all turned towards the shattered bottles and glasses. They were distracted by the commotion for a second, but it was a fateful second.

One screamed, "What in tarnation?" He paused as his eyes went from the unbelievable sight to reaching for his pistol.

Jonas swung the smoking barrels towards the outlaws and fired. The shotgun was deadly at this range. It spewed its buckshot and fire like some kind of small dragon. The four ruffians next to him all crumpled to the floor.

Jonas dropped the shotgun and flipped the left side of the borrowed coat back where the other shotgun hung from a wire loop. He lifted it free and fired into Winters and the man standing next to him. Both staggered and fell backward with a load of lead buried in their bodies.

Morrison screamed, "Tex! He got Tex and the other boys! He even got the boss!"

Morrison was in a total state of panic, which was not unusual. What was unexpected, was that everyone else was panicking, as well.

Jonas fired the new weapon from his hip and two more fell. Now the three outlaws who remained standing returned fire, but Jonas slipped back behind the end of the bar. Huge chunks of the bar flew through the air and those projectiles that passed went wildly out the door.

The black smoke rose to the ceiling, but it couldn't rise fast enough and soon became like a cloud that was blotting out the sun.

One of the tables in the saloon flipped over. Like the glasses before, it seemed as if some unseen hand had turned it over. It strangely slid to the end of the bar. Jonas stuck the barrel between the end of the bar and the convenient table and fired in the direction of those who were attacking him. He flipped back and pulled four rounds from the buffalo coat, slipping two into the now empty chambers and sticking two in his mouth. He glanced around the corner and saw the other shotgun laying a few feet from him. He tried to reach it but several rounds from the gang forced him to pull back. He let out a cuss and was shocked when the abandoned shotgun slid across the short distance and all he had to do was grasp the barrel and pull it behind the bar.

He broke it open and reloaded it. Although he was in a fight like he hadn't been in in years, he smiled. The feeling of being invincible crept over him. He knew he had far more than firepower working for him.

The remaining outlaws all fired. The bullets flew everywhere, but Jonas managed to stay securely behind the bar. Like the experienced gunfighter he was, he waited for the lull and then stood. His first shot took the hat and half of the face off a man trying to reload. His next round missed as the remaining men flew behind anything that could protect them from the onslaught of death.

Morrison was one of the few remaining men. He had always been known as the talker and not a fighter. He shouted, "This ain't right! None of this is right! How is Flannigan doing any of this? And why does it seem like he's got God almighty on his side?"

As Jonas pushed two new rounds into the shotgun, he shouted back from behind the bar, "I ain't got the Good Lord on my side, Morrison. But what I've got's plenty good enough for me."

Jonas swung from the cover as he heard the thunder of boots running for the door and fired. The shot struck Morrison flush in the face. Parts of his skin flew off, and blood sprayed onto the wall on the other side of the room. When Morrison skidded across the floor, even people who had ridden with him for months wouldn't have been able to recognize what remained.

One of the men shouted, "He's a demon! A damn demon, that's what he is! He's fighting like a man possessed!"

Jonas shouted at the top of his voice as he replaced

the fired cartridges, "A man possessed, eh? Ha! You wouldn't believe how right you are."

The outlaws were all stunned when he stood and waded towards them. Fire was flying from both shotguns and the room was now so full of smoke and the smell of gunpowder that it was hard to breathe. Jonas' first two shots were devastating, and it left three more outlaws dead. The last three ruffians ran toward the door. Jonas fired both barrels and two crashed to the floor.

The last remaining gangster shouted, "Damn, I've gotta get out of here! You're crazy!"

Jumping over the bodies of his companions, he started to run out of the saloon. Jonas quickly reloaded the shotgun.

Just as the man reached the saloon's swinging doors, Brother George threw his shoulder into them from the outside. The runner staggered backward. His eyes were glued to the door and he stood for a second. He shook his head and ran back toward the door. Before he reached it, Jonas fired. This time, George stepped away and the man's body fell through the batwings.

"That's the last of 'em," Jonas said.

Jameson said, "That was amazing! I never knew that I could actually move objects in this state!" He was excited and enthusiastic, after he had smashed up the saloon. He never knew he could do anything like that, until Kennedy told him.

"I didn't know that I could possess bodies either, Jack. The old shaman taught me things about what we can and can't do as spirits. Good thing Jonas allowed me to possess his body. He would never have managed to shoot down all those no-accounts, much less gather enough guts to steal those sawed-off shotguns and ammo from the gun store."

He laughed. "But didn't he look good in my coat? If he'd been filled out, those shotguns would've never fit under it."

It was Kennedy. He was speaking through Jonas' body, and he could see Jameson plainly. "All the difference in the world after Spirit Speaker showed me the things us spirits can do. You did a great job smashing those bottles, and you slid me that table and shotgun exactly when I needed them."

Jameson said, "You sure handled them well. I kind of guess one of the reasons was that they was spooked, because of the way Jonas came at 'em."

Kennedy said, "Might have been. You also could say that he had every right to be spooked by the spooks. After it's all said and done, there was no way I was going down twice to that no-account Bundy. He had already killed me once. I wasn't going to let him kill Jonas. After all, his body was just on loan."

CHAPTER NINE

The bodies of Bundy and his gang were buried in shallow graves outside of town. They were given the last rites, and their graves had markers, just like everyone else. They were bad men, but the townspeople of Angel were not the vindictive sort. They were decent folk to the core. They definitely didn't deserve it, but that was just the way the people of Angel were.

"Where are you going to go now, Jonas?" Jameson asked.

Kennedy and Jameson were standing beside Jonas. They each had an arm on his shoulder. Jonas was physically a changed man. His clothes were spotless, and he was clean shaven. His parted hair lay smooth and trimmed. Instead of the smell of whiskey, the sweet aroma of lilac water filled the air.

Kennedy said, "I guess you told the town council that you'd take the job as sheriff."

"If I'da had to do it alone, I'd've had to've turned it down. But after Jameson said he'd stay right here at my side and George said he also wanted to help, I felt like I could handle it. Ya know, back years ago, I was a good hand with a rifle or a pistol. It was just the loss of my brother that sent me a little crazy and the whiskey helped me feel better. Brother George visiting me after he was dead is what made it easy for you guys to come along."

Kennedy dropped his hand from Jonas' shoulder. Smiling at him, Kennedy said, "You know that I'm on call any time Jameson or you need me to back your play. I'd stay now, but I've got to go see Spirit Speaker. I owe him, and I know he'll be calling me to pay my debt any day now." His smile faded and he continued, "Jonas, you keep a watchful eye on Betsy for me. I only wish I could take her with me. I'd like to hope that one of the things Spirit Speaker can teach me is how to make love to a woman that you miss more than the morning sun. That might be asking too much, but in time, I might find peace."

Jonas nodded and smiled at Kennedy. "That's good to hear, Marshal. Me and Jack here can take care of Angel while you're gone. It's going to be tough rebuilding the town after all the chaos and mayhem that Bundy and his crew unleashed. Still, I'm sure that Jack and I can handle it. Besides the people of Angel are tough as cow hide. I know they'll bounce back from this."

Kennedy smiled at them. "I don't doubt that, Jonas. I don't doubt that at all, but just in case you need an extra hand, you know I'll be here."

"You take care of yourself, Marshal," Jameson said sincerely.

"Likewise for you both, Jack. Oh, and one more thing..."

"What's that?"

Kennedy smiled at Jack. "You were right. I should have made you my deputy."

Jack chuckled and nodded. With that, Kennedy turned around and started walking. Jonas watched him walk into the horizon. As quickly as he had appeared, he vanished into the blazing rays of the sun. Jonas turned to where Kennedy had been standing. There was nothing but the shimmering of the leaves as the tree appeared to be trembling from the speed of his departure.

Jonas scratched his head. He took a deep breath and looked down the main street of Angel. He smiled and nodded. "I sure am gonna give this a try. Jameson and Marshal Kennedy, you may have made a new man out of me."

CHAPTER TEN

"There is no doubt I owe you, Sprit Speaker, and I'm sure you called me back to tell me what I must do for you." Marshal Kennedy bowed his head before the shaman.

"You aren't as slow as many a white eye. Yes, you do owe me and what I ask is something that I know you can do."

Kennedy nodded. "If it can be done, I promise you it will be."

Spirit Speaker pulled the whiskey bottle to his lips and turned it up. Kennedy could see bubbles drifting toward the bottom as the liquid drained. The shaman slowly withdrew the bottle and blew out a small amount of air.

"There is something happening at the military headquarters. Colonel Baker has received a large shipment of supplies that are meant for my people, and he also has received a herd of cattle that is meant for us. It has long been known that he has stolen from our allotment, and I fear that it will happen again. I don't know if my people can survive another year of short rations. I don't know what you can do, but if you value what I have done for you, you will find a way."

"Send me. If it can be done it will be."

***

The colonel's office was guarded by a private with a Sharps held against his chest. Kennedy smiled as he walked past him and slipped through the door. He assumed that the officer sitting behind the desk was Colonel Baker, but was confused, as another officer with the same rank sat facing Baker.

"Baker, I have delivered the twenty wagons of supplies to you. If you would like, my men and I can take them on to the village. I don't think it would be any problem for us to drive that herd of cows at the same time."

"Colonel Jenkins, I have other plans, but I appreciate your offer."

Jenkins leaned back in his chair. "Baker, it will be no problem, and I can't understand what other plans you might have for the supplies."

Baker's face reddened, his eyes narrowed, and he pitched forward in his chair. "Are you questioning my authority to do as I please with what's been brought to my command? As we discussed at lunch, I outrank you by two months, and therefore I resent you even thinking about questioning my actions."

Colonel Jenkins drew his lips into a hard line. "I'm sorry, it is just that I was raised by a father who spent all of his life as a missionary to an Indian tribe in Iowa, and I know that these folks have been promised supplies and promised fair treatment and seem never to received it. I am committed to seeing that they get their fair due."

"Jenkins, I spent five miserable years fighting the red sons-of-bitches, and I have no love for their kind. They have pillaged and burned many a settler, and they have ambushed many a patrol. Blood of the white man is their total game. They played it and now it is time they pay for it. As a matter of fact, it doesn't bother me one bit to make them suffer and at the same time make a profit."

"What the hell are you saying? I am an officer and sworn to complete my orders. My orders were to deliver the wagons for the Indians, and I have a feeling that that is not going to happen. I am appalled at your response and now I am greatly concerned for the wellbeing of those who you were supposed to be caring for. They may have fought us, but they have surrendered, and an agreement was reached in that process. Now, as gentlemen and officers, we are supposed to uphold that agreement."

Kennedy stood and watched as the two officers' conversation got tenser. He leaned back against the wall and observed with great interest.

Baker rose from behind the desk and put both fists on the top of his desk as he leaned toward Jenkins. "I am in command here and what I say goes. I'm ordering you to take your men and get off my post!"

Jenkins stood and stepped back. "I am leaving as ordered, but I promise you that this isn't the end of this."

Kennedy watched as Jenkins turned on his heel and made his way out the door. He hesitated for a moment and watched Baker. It dawned on him that Jenkins was the one he should keep an eye on. He already knew what scum Baker was. The conversation had confirmed everything that Spirit Speaker had said.

He turned and walked through the closed door. He saw Jenkins entering the headquarters office and rushed to observe what was happening. To save time, he walked through the wall as Jenkins was giving orders to the telegraph operator.

Jenkins was bent over the desk and the quill was rapidly going from the paper to the ink well. He was cussing as he wrote.

Turning to the telegraph operator, he barked, "Send this immediately to General Crook. Mark it urgent!"

"Yes, sir!" was followed by a salute, and the corporal fell to the telegraph key like it was the last drink in town. The tapping sounded like a flock of chickens trying to get the last kernels of corn lying on a tin can. When the corporal finished, he looked up at Colonel Jenkins. "It's sent, sir."

"Good. I'm going to my tent. You will immediately bring me the reply."

"Yes, sir!"

Kennedy shook his head. He decided to just wait by the telegraph. Whatever was going to happen was going to be started right in front of him.

In less than an hour, the tapping commenced. It seemed faster than usual and the corporal was writing like it was his last will and testament and he was getting ready to face a firing squad. He would let out a cuss every few lines.

Kennedy could tell by his reactions that what he was getting was full of shocking commands. When the tapping stopped, the corporal shouted to an empty room, "Good Lord, I can't believe this!"

He pulled on his hat and straightened his bandana. Pulling the paper to his chest, he ran out the door. Kennedy followed him through the door as it swung shut. The corporal ran to Jenkins' tent. He stumbled to an erect stance and shouted, "Message for the colonel!"

"Enter!"

He stooped and entered the large tent. Kennedy walked through the wall. "Sir, the message is as follows. Have Colonel Baker immediately stand down. Colonial Jenkins to take command of the post. Full delivery of all food stuffs, supplies to be delivered post haste."

Jenkins said, "Thank you, Corporal. Get a sergeant and Major Wilson, and come with me. You will read the instructions to Colonel Baker."

"Yes, sir!"

In less than ten minutes, the four-man entourage was

gathered at the door to Colonel Baker's office. The private stepped back as they entered. Kennedy walked through the wall. He was starting to enjoy this part of being dead.

When they entered, Baker rose from his desk. His face was gnarled, and his eyes looked as if he was trying to burn a hole through the group. "What the hell are you doing here, Jenkins? I ordered you to leave. And what are the rest of you men doing, besides abandoning your posts? I should have you all court martialed for dereliction of duty."

Jenkins stepped forward. "Colonel Baker, the corporal has a message from General Crook, and I have asked him to deliver it to you."

The corporal's hand was shaking as he held the paper in front of him. He cleared his throat twice and took a deep breath. "General Crook has ordered that Colonel Baker step down from his command position and that Colonel Jenkins is to take full command of the post. He states that a full hearing will be held into matters of the operation of the post over the past two years."

The color drained from Baker's face. He first stooped over and then he rose to full height. He made a snappy right turn and took three quick steps to past the end of his desk. A brisk left turn followed. He stood motionless for a moment, then shouted, "You son-of-a-bitch, Jenkins!"

He flipped the flap on his pistol's holster and grabbed the handle. As the gun cleared the holster, Kennedy kicked the table in front of him with all his force. It struck Baker in the legs, and he pitched forward. As he was falling to the floor, his pistol exploded and a bloody hole appeared in the top of his head.

The men stood in silence for a moment, looking at one another. Major Wilson gingerly stepped over to Baker and turned him over. "Good Lord, he's dead."

More silence.

Jenkins finally said, "Well, that saved the army some awkwardness."

The corporal looked at Jenkins. "Excuse me, sir, but how did you kick that table?"

Jenkins said, "I thought you kicked it."

"No, sir. I didn't do a thing."

Jenkins chuckled. "Huh. Guess it must have been a ghost."

THE END

About This Author

Dylan Johnson likes apples. Especially made into apple pie served vanilla ice cream. Dylan Johnson likes baseball—especially the Dodgers. Dylan Johnson loves Marty Robbins. Marty has the voice of the cowboy. A voice he heard his whole life. Working as a writer has been one of the great experiences of Dylan's life. Being married to Sarah-Lee has been one of the great experiences of Dylan's life. Going to church each Sunday and praising the Lord is one of his favorite things to do. Dylan Johnson is a Christian, married writer who loves Marty Robbins, the Dodgers and apple pie. What more can you ask for?

Dylan's favorite authors are Louis L'Amour, William Johnstone, Cherokee Parks, Scott Harris, Johnny Gunn, Neville Shute, J.C. Hulsey and Irving Wallace.

Made in the USA
Middletown, DE
28 May 2019